At One
In a place called Maine

written by Lynn Plourde
ILLUSTRATIONS BY Leslie Mansmann

ISLANDPORT PRESS

ISLANDPORT PRESS

Islandport Press
P.O. Box 10
Yarmouth, Maine 04096
info@islandportpress.com
www.islandportpress.com

Text copyright © Lynn Plourde
Illustrations copyright © 2007 Leslie Mansmann
All rights reserved. No part of this book may be reproduced
in any manner without the express written consent of
Islandport Press, except in the case of brief excerpts in
critical reviews and articles.

Revised printing, 2021

ISBN: 1-978-1-934031-06-3
Library of Congress Control Number: 2007929671
Printed in China
Job # 2021080622

To Maine, the perfect place for me
—Lynn Plourde

To Patricia and Margaret
—Leslie Mansmann

At One
In a place called Maine

WRITTEN BY Lynn Plourde
ILLUSTRATIONS BY Leslie Mansmann

I live in a place
where I sit still, so still,
upon a stone wall in my back yard.

I am at one
with twin fawns
stopping for an early morning snack
offered by outstretched apple tree arms.

I live in a place
where I stand tall, so tall,
as I balance on boulders.

I am at one
with a mighty mountain,
reaching and arching
to touch the clouds
just a pinch away.

I live in a place
where I frolic playfully, so playfully,
amongst a red, gold, orange
confetti of leaves.

I am at one
with autumn's
wild and wondrous celebration.

I live in a place
where I bound boldly, so boldly,
along the craggy shore.

I am at one
with the crashing, dashing waves
as they bellow and boast
of their power and beauty.

I live in a place
where I awaken sparked, so sparked
as the first light ignites.

I am at one
with the radiant dawn,
a pink-orange fire
that flickers and flashes,
flaring up a new day.

I live in a place
where I peek curiously, so curiously,
out at a darkness lit by fireflies.

I am at one
with the snooping black bear
who sniffs and snorts the tent,
snuffling for treats,
before moseying along
with a goodbye garumph.

I live in a place
where I rest gratefully, so gratefully,
upon a rock blanket
after a hot, humid hike.

I am at one
with the rumbling, tumbling waterfall
that changes sweat to chills
with its shower of splatters and sprinkles.

I live in a place
where I breathe deeply, so deeply,
a forest potpourri.

I am at one
with spiky pines
that circle and scent the air
with their evergreen, everlasting
Christmas tree smell.

I live in a place
where I ride slowly, so slowly,
along a winding, twining dirt road.

I am at one
with a carefree, meandering moose
whose only concern
is a munchy, marshy lunch.

I live in a place
where I glide gently, so gently,
creating crisscross designs
across a fresh canvas of snow.

I am at one
with the shadowy ice sculptures
and windswept swirling drifts
of winter's moonlit mural.

I live in a place
called Maine
where I live proudly, so proudly,
where the coast melts into the sea,

where mountains
merge with the sky,

where forests and fields
are stitched together by streams and rivers
creating a quilted landscape;

a place
where nature
welcomes all
to share its beauty
and its space,
to touch its heartbeat,
to thrive,
to breathe,
to live . . .

at one.

About the Author

Lynn Plourde was born in Dexter, Maine, and raised in Skowhegan. She is the author of more than fifteen books for children, including *Pigs in the Mud in the Middle of the Rud* (her first), *Dino Pets, Teacher Appreciation Day, The First Feud: Between the Mountain and the Sea,* and *Merry Moosey Christmas*.

Her books have won both regional and national awards. *At One* is a love letter to her home state of Maine and lyrically celebrates its inspirational beauty from the wilds of Baxter State Park to the crashing waves of the Atlantic.

Plourde is a graduate of the University of Maine and worked for twenty-one years as a speech therapist in Maine public schools. In addition to writing books, Plourde makes many author visits to Maine schools to work with young students and presents workshops and seminars to professionals. She now lives in Winthrop.

About the Illustrator

Leslie Mansmann earned her illustration degree at the Philadelphia College of Art and has spent the past thirty years working as a freelance illustrator. She illustrated her first children's book *When I'm With You* in 2003. She has also provided illustrations for John McDonald's *down the road a piece: A Storyteller's Guide to Maine*.

Mansmann's other work includes creating a poster series for J. Weston Walsh that is part of a nationwide English and writing educational campaign, and illustrating a set of exclusive prints for Sturbridge Yankee Workshop. She lives in North Yarmouth, Maine, with her husband and three children as well as her cats, dogs, and horses.

For *At One*, Mansmann employed a painting style that features gouache, an opaque watercolor that allows for more vibrant, bold colors and cleaner lines than those found in traditional watercolors.